Hood Chick
Delivered

Hood Chick
Delivered

SHATERRA GENTRY

**J. KENKADE
PUBLISHING**™

A division of J. Kenkade Enterprises, LLC

Hood Chick Delivered
Copyright © 2017 by Shaterra Gentry

J. Kenkade Publishing
6104 Forbing Rd
Little Rock, AR 72209
www.jkenkade.com
Facebook.com/JKenkade

J. Kenkade Publishing is an imprint of
J. Kenkade Enterprises, LLC.
The J. Kenkade Publishing name and logo
are trademarks of J. Kenkade Enterprises, LLC.

Printed in the United States of America
ISBN 978-1-944486-77-8

*This book is dedicated to my late cousin
Desmond Rashun Smith aka Chapo*

Contents

Chapter 1
Mrs. Roxy's Return

ॐ

Sasha and Layna were in the car riding when Sasha got a phone call.

Ring. Ring. Ring.

"Hello!?" Sasha answered.

"Hey, this Roxy. Where you at?" Roxy said.

"Roxy, Mrs. Roxy—badass Roxy?" Sasha replied.

"Sasha yes! It's me! Where Layna at?" Roxy yelled.

"We on the southside finna hit up Plug J's house." Sasha replied.

"Roxy out! I'll see ya'll in a few minutes," Roxy said maliciously.

"Man Layna… you'll never guess who that was on my phone." Sasha said.

"Sasha, I heard your conversation. Why that chick Roxy want to see us?" Layna said angrily.

Sasha replied, "I don't know girl. We was cool before she did that bid."

"Sasha that chick is up to something. You got your strap?" Layna said seriously.

She raised her shirt up.

Sasha replied, "Chick I stay ready. Let her try some slick crap if she wants to." "Ladies, ladies, ladies…how do I get so lucky to have both of you fine ass ladies in my house."

J said jokingly.

"Cut the crap J. You know exactly why me and Layna here." Sasha said with attitude.

"Damn shawty, why you always gotta treat me like that?" J asked.

Sasha rolled her eyes and said, "P.J. cut the small talk. You got the crap I need or not?!"

"Since you want to act like that, I do. Y'all got my money?" J replied.

"Layna show that nigga that bag before I slap him." Sasha said rolling her eyes again.

"Girl stop talking to him like that. That's why nobody wants to work with us now." Layna said loudly.

"It's okay shawty. Sasha knows I'll do anything for her chocolate ass. I don't care how mean she is." J said as he walked off.

Smiling, Sasha said, "J get the products for me,

then I gotta set-up some stuff."

J replied "Okay baby girl. I'll be right back."

Bump. Bump.

Sasha jumped and asked, "Layna! You hear that crap? What was that?"

Layna replied, "Girl I don't know… probably a rat or something— you know this trap old."

"Heeyyy chicks!" Roxy said walking through the door.

Sasha and Layna looked at each other in awe. No words could come to them.

"Y'all look like y'all seen a damn ghost. What's up?" Roxy said laughing.

"H-hey Roxy," Sasha said.

"Layna I know you heard me speak to you twice," Roxy said looking at Layna. "Roxy I ain't got to say crap to you if I don't want to," Layna snapped.

"To be so sweet little wanch you got a smart-ass mouth." Roxy said.

"Cut the crap Roxy. What you want and why you want to see me and Sasha?" Layna asked.

"Well damn little mama. Me and Sasha was pretty cool before I went away." Roxy explained.

"I was telling her that Roxy, but what you got up your sleeve?" Sasha said quickly. Roxy answered, "I don't have anything up my sleeve. Why y'all so paranoid?" "Roxy, we know how you rock and we don't want no parts in it. We stay lowkey for a reason," Sasha said angrily.

"Listen Sasha, chick you owe me. You gonna do what I say do." Roxy said with her finger in Sasha's face.

"But...but," Sasha tried to say.

"*But* my ass! You heard what I said," Roxy said with attitude.

Plug J walked back in and said, "Ladies I got your—"

He saw Roxy, stopped and asked, "What y'all got going and why she in my house?"

"Damn what's up J!? You not happy to see me either?" Roxy asked smiling.

J replied, "Aye shawty, I don't really rock with you like that and if you gonna conduct business with them, you can wait outside when we finish."

"Alright, alright. I'll respect that. Sasha I'll see your ass outside," Roxy said maliciously.

Sasha just stared wondering why out of all people, Roxy thought she 'owed' her.

"Aye baby girl. What that chick got going on and why she talking to you like that?" J asked.

Sasha stumbled and replied, "I-I don't know J, but I'm gonna find out."

J said angrily, "If she on some bull crap baby

girl, I'll take care of the old chick for you."

Sasha hugged J and said, "Thanks J. I will. Layna, let me talk to this woman and see what she wants."

Layna replied with anger, "I ain't leaving you alone with her ass."

Sasha said calmly, "Layna, go. I'm good."

"Hey chick, you hurt my best friend and the problems you gonna have you ain't gonna want." Layna threatened.

"Bye Layna girl. I'm gonna take care of Sasha," Roxy replied laughing.

"I'll call you later Layna," Sasha said.

"Okay, you better call!" Layna said looking at Roxy.

Roxy said, "Come tomorrow at three and I'll tell you everything you need to know."

"Okay Roxy!" Sasha replied.

Sasha walked to her car and called Layna.

Ring. Ring.

"Layna!" Sasha yelled.

"What that chick want?" Layna asked.

"She's talking about 'meet her at Peezy's place tomorrow at three," Sasha explained.

"Why Sasha?" Layna asked.

"I don't know Layna. She said she would tell me when I got there," Sasha replied. "Alright,

I'm going with you. Come on over so we can get these products together," Layna demanded.

"Alright I'm headed your way girl." Sasha replied hanging up.

Chapter 2
The Meet Up
(Peezy's Place)

❧

A ye bro. What's good witcha?

This was how Kid Fresh and John-John greeted each other.

"Man… dog I found this *fly* chick. I think she may be good for you," John-John said as they dapped.

"John-John these females ain't finna act right. I don't need these chicks,"

Kid said seriously.

"Kid you can't just call all females *chicks*. There's some good ones still around," John-John stressed.

"Bro I don't want to hear that!" Kid said throwing his hands up.

John-John said seriously, "If you go for these thot-dressing, club-hopping chicks what you expect Kid?"

"Aye my niggas, what y'all got going on?" Ant Dog said.

Together John-John and Kid said, "Ant Dogg!"

"Aye Ant, tell this nigga Kid all females ain't bad," John-John said.

"John-John… chicks ain't loyal no more. Kid right. Forget these chicks," Ant replied.

"Man, I don't know what's wrong with y'all. Both of y'all trippin'," John-John expressed.

Ant Dog gave Kid a look and said, "Watch this nigga John-John. Since these chicks so good, why yo' ugly-ass single like us?"

Laughing, John-John said, "Man I'm single because unlike you niggas, I'm looking for a woman that's on her crap— scraping tryna' run up a check."

Ant Dog laughed and said, "Bro, I got crap to do. Can't be listening to your Shakespeare raping ass."

"Alright. Ant Dog, holler at you later dog," Kid said.

"Y'all niggas gonna start listening to my ass, but aite my dude." John-John said. "Knock, knock."

"Aye who is it?" John-John said.

"Sasha and Layna!" Sasha said with attitude.

"Aye bro. Layna is the girl I was talking about for you," John-John said.

Kid said rolling his eyes, "Whatever bro. Let them chicks in."

John-John opened the door and asked, "Hey, what can I help you with?"

"Hey John-John!" Layna said.

"What's up shorty? You good?" John-John replied.

"Yea I'm good. Where Roxy's ass at?" Layna said.

"She's not here yet, but I bet Peezy knows where and how long it will take her to get here." John-John said.

"Alright get her, then me and Sasha got crap to do," Layna said angrily.

"Be right back shortly," John-John said walking off.

"You're a little feisty aren't you shorty?" Kid asked.

"Who the hell are you— shorty forty?" Layna snapped.

"Damn shorty! I'm Kid Fresh. May I ask you something?" Kid said.

"I'd wish you wouldn't, but since I'm feeling nice what's up?" Layna said sarcastically.

"To be so pretty, why you have to act so ugly?" Kid asked.

Layna snapped, "Nigga it's because you niggas

made me this way. Now don't ask me crap else."

Peezy walked up and said, "What's up? What y'all need?"

"Roxy told me to meet her here at three today," Sasha replied.

"What's your name shawty?" Peezy asked.

"Sasha." Sasha answered.

"Okay, okay! Come to my office." Peezy said walking toward her office.

"Aye I'm coming too bro!" Layna said.

"Who is that?" Peezy asked.

"That's my partner!" Sasha replied.

"Partner... *girlfriend* 'partner'?" Peezy asked.

Sasha looked crazy and replied, "No! My *business* partner Layna."

Pezzy shrugged her shoulders and said, "Oh alright. You can come too shawty." (Gets to the office.)

"Y'all come on in and close the door."

As Layna and Sasha sit down, the chair behind the desk turns around and it is Roxy.

Laughing, Roxy says, "I didn't think you'd be brave enough to show up Sasha." Sasha snapped, "I'm here ain't I? Cut the small talk. What you want!"

"Well baby girl, I got a proposition for you. I think you'd like it."

Sasha rolled her eyes and said, "Roxy get to the crap. I got things to do."

"Sasha you know I don't like to be rushed," Roxy said.

Sasha looked upside Roxy's head and said, "My time is valuable also."

"Alright! Alright! I'm partnering with Peezy with this strip club. You want to make some extra cash or not?" Roxy quickly said.

"Roxy... I don't know about all that crap. I'll think about it and get back with you." Sasha replied.

"Girl don't think too long. I ain't gonna hold the position open long," Roxy said knowing the spot would be open because no one else wanted it.

"Yea, yea. Layna let's go!" Sasha said.

"Hey Layna, I could use you and that plump ass of yours too," Roxy said jokingly. "Chick get a life! I'll never work for you," Layna snarled.

Roxy laughed and said, "Ha! Layna, you don't have to treat me like that."

"Bye chick!" Layna said with as much attitude as she could.

Chapter 3

The Talk

❧

As soon as Sasha and Layna walked out of Peezy's place, they began to talk about what just happened.

With attitude Layna said, "Sasha I know damn well you're not thinking about dancing again."

Sasha said sadly, "Layna, don't start. You know I'm only thinking I ain't finna do that again."

"Bull crap! I can see it in your face. You want to!" Layna said angrily.

"Okay! I want to, but I don't at the same time!" Sasha snapped back.

"You know what happened last time!?" Layna said angrily.

"I know Layna, but I'm older and wiser now. Plus I made good money," Sasha said trying to reason with Layna.

"All that sounds good, but your life is way more important than that cash," Layna said concerned.

"Promise me, if I do start back dancing, you won't judge me and stop being my friend," Sasha said with tears in her eyes.

Layna replied, "Sasha I'll never judge you or stop being your friend. I love you too much."

With relief Sasha said, "Thank you girl. I love you too. I was scared you'd hate me for even thinking about it."

Laughing, Layna said, "Girl I knew when you told her you'd think about it that you wanted to."

"Can you really blame me? I don't want to slang for the rest of my life." Sasha said curiously.

"Sasha I support anything you do, and I understand I don't want to slang forever either," Layna replied.

"Well Layna, you have the best body. Why won't you just dance too?" Sasha said.

"I almost slapped you. I will never work with Roxy's ass," Layna snapped.

"Okay Layna okay. I'm finna head to the crib. You coming or not?" Sasha said. "Naw babe. I got some business to handle. I'll call you later," Layna replied.

"Okay, I love you girl!" Sasha said walking off.

"Love you too," Layna replied.

Chapter 4

The Run In

John-John and Kid met up to have a guy's talk.

"Bro she was mad fine. She looks like she got a little hood in her," Kid said.

"Kid I told you, but all you wanted to do was talk crazy about chicks," John-John said seriously.

"Well nigga you didn't tell me what shawty was working with," Kid said laughing. "It ain't all about looks Kid. It's about what kind of head she has on her shoulders," John-John replied.

"Let me stop you there. John-John…nigga I'm looking for a hood chick with good sex. What you mean?" Kid said rubbing his hands together.

"Let me get this straight bro. All you basically want is a chick that can sex you good that can slang and shoot a gun?" John-John asked looking disgusted.

Very seriously, Kid said, "Hell yea my nigga!"

"Answer me this… how you going to build

something with a chick like that?" John-John asked seriously.

"Nigga, easy. If we both slanging, we good," Kid answered.

"Man Kid, you shouldn't want yo' shawty on these dirty streets," John-John said shaking his head.

Both Kid and John-John stop mid-conversation as Layna walked by.

"Hey John-John!" Layna said.

"Hey Layna, you alright ma'?" John-John replied.

"I'm good. You aite bro?" Layna said.

"Yea, I'm boss sis. What you finna get into?" John-John asked.

"Gotta bust a few moves. Then I'm going to hit up the crib. You?" Layna replied. "Same 'ole same 'ole sis. You know all I do is grind." John-John replied.

"I know, I know." Layna said.

"I don't mean to be rude. This is my homie, Kid," John-John said.

Kid said, "What's up shawty? Nice to meet you."

Rolling her eyes Layna said, "Hi! Same here!"

Quickly John-John said, "Alright fam. I'm finna head out. Y'all be good."

"John-John where you going?" Layna said.

"Got to find Ant. I'll call you later love," he said walking off.

"Alright bro, be good," Kid said

"Fasho'!" John-John yelled back.

Layna began to walk off.

"Say lil' mama!" Kid yelled.

Layna turned around and said, "First off, don't approach me like that thug. If you gonna talk to me, address me by my name!"

"I'm sorry shawty. My fault," Kid apologized.

"You right. Now what you want 'Kid'? Why they call you that anyway?" Layna said.

Kid went into detail, "Well shawty, I've been on this game since I was a pup. So *Kid Fresh* just stuck with me. My pops kept me fresh in the latest."

"Oh okay. Now what was your reason for trying to get my attention?" Layna asked.

"Well honestly you seem like a pretty cool shawty. Anyone that vibes with John-John has to be cool people," Kid said.

"You babbling! Just tell me what you want boss," Layna interrupted.

"Dang shawty. My bad. I just want to get to know you is all," Kid said raising his hands.

"I don't know about all that, but give me ya' info and I may contact you!" Layna said as she handed Kid her phone.

"Alright shawty, whenever you feel the need hit me up…" Kid replied.

"Aye you don't have to tell me. I will." Layna said with an attitude.

"Later shawty!" Kid replied.

"I'll holler at you boss," Layna said as she walked off and immediately called Sasha.

Ring…Ring.

"Hey Layna. What's up girl?" Sasha answered.

"Girl you'd never guess who I ran into a while ago." Layna said.

"Who girl?" Sasha asked.

"Kid Fresh and John-John, girl. John-John thought he was slick gonna play like he had to make some jump and leave me with Kid alone," Layna said rolling her eyes. "Ha! Girl did you run the boy off?" Sasha asked laughing.

"See there!" Layna said upset.

"I'm sorry Layna, but you can be a *chick* sometimes." Sasha said softly.

"You didn't have to say that Sasha. Damn, I wasn't that mean to him. I took his number," Layna said sadly.

Sasha said excitedly, "OOOOOWWWWWEEE! Girl you gonna call him?"

"I'm not thirsty. I'll let his mind wonder and

I'll hit him up in a few days," Layna said angrily.

"Okay miss *hard-to-get*," Sasha said sarcastically.

"No! It's *miss-not-easy*. That's what these niggas think flashing ice and cash can get them—anybody," Layna snapped back.

"Well girl, you know I love me a man with a whole lot of cash and ice. It's a must," Sasha said licking her tongue out.

"Girl that's why you're single and battered. Now these thugs ain't caring about us." Layna stressed.

"Anyway Layna, I gotta go. I'll talk to you later," Sasha said with an attitude.

"Sasha, you don't—" Layna tried to say.

Click!

"That chick hung up on me!" Layna thought out loud.

Chapter 5

A Day at Peezy's Place

❧

"Hey Roxy! Roxy! Oh, you can't hear me?" Peezy screamed.

"I'm sorry Peezy. I was thinking about something," Roxy exclaimed.

"Well chick, think when you're not working. What that chick Sasha say she was gonna do?" Peezy said.

"I…I haven't heard from her P," Roxy stumbled to say.

Angrily Peezy said, "Chick didn't I tell you to have her in here by Friday?" she said walking up in Roxy's face.

"P it's only Wednesday," Roxy said trying not to fall over the chair.

"Well chick, you got two days. She better be here!" Peezy threatened.

"I'll make sure she does, okay?" Roxy said

softly.

"Yea get out my office with your ugly-ass!" Peezy yelled.

Roxy opened the door and loud music was playing.

"Girl, you look good. Want you to back that ass up!"

"Roxy! Roxy!" Sugar yelled.

"Sugar what you want!" Roxy yelled back.

"Why you got tears in your eyes? You okay?" Sugar asked.

"I'm fine sugar. Is that all you want!?" Roxy yelled.

"No, Roxy. I need your advice." Sugar replied.

"What's up?" Roxy asked.

"Well, I've been thinking about getting back into school so I can get out of this place, but I'm scared I'm not smart enough." Sugar said sadly.

"Sugar, I'm gonna tell you like this— if you never try something you will never know how good you'll be at it." Roxy said gracefully.

"You got a point, but dancing is all I know." Sugar said holding her head down. "Sugar, chase your dreams. Do them until you figure out if you really want to leave here." Roxy pleaded.

"Thank you, Roxy!" Sugar said hugging Roxy.

"Now go shake some ass. I need $4000 out of

you tonight." Roxy said smiling.

"I won't promise you that, but I'll try. You know Wednesday's are not my nights?" Sugar said.

"Make them your nights. Do what you got to do Sugar. You think too much." Roxy said.

"Alright Roxy! See you at closing. Roxy walked outside to call Sasha.

Ring... Ring.

"Hello! Sasha!" Roxy yelled.

"Who is this!" Sasha yelled back.

"Sasha, this Roxy." Roxy replied.

"Do you see how late it is? What you want Roxy!?" Sasha said angrily.

"I just want your answer." Roxy said softly.

"Could you not have called me in the morning?" Sasha asked.

"I mean I could've, but we on the phone right now." Roxy said.

"Roxy... I told you I would think about it. Why you pressuring me!?" Sasha yelled.

"Because I know you want to. I don't know why you acting like you don't." Roxy said slickly.

"Roxy, let me make that decision!" Sasha said angrily.

"I am... I am. I'm just saying..." Roxy calmly said.

"Well I'll call you later today with my decision.

Is that okay?" Sasha said

"Yes, I'll be waiting. Don't take all day." Roxy said maliciously.

"Bye Roxy!" Sasha said.

"Bye!" Roxy said as she walked back in the building.

"Throw that ass in a circle, throw that ass in a circle."

Knock. Knock.

The office door swung open.

"Bring your ass in here, and you better have good news bothering me!" Peezy yelled.

"Peezy I… I called Sasha." Roxy began to say.

"Cut it chick. Did she say yes or no!" Peezy snapped.

"Well neither." Roxy replied.

"How you got good news? I should slap yo' ass!" Peezy threatened.

Roxy yelled, "No Peezy!"

"Give me a reason I shouldn't!" Peezy said angrily.

"She's gonna call me with her answer later today!" Roxy yelled as she jumped back. "If the answer is not yes chick, you better figure out a way to make her say yes!" Peezy said pushing Roxy.

"Okay, okay!" Roxy yelled.

"Out my face chick!" Peezy said.

At this time, it was time to go home at 7 a.m.

Ring.

"Hello...hello?" Roxy said quickly.

"Dang Roxy. You gonna let the phone ring." Sasha said laughing.

"I— it did Sasha." Roxy stuttered.

"Why you sound like you're scared for your life?" Sasha asked concerned.

"Chick, what's the answer?" Roxy snapped.

"Roxy if you gonna talk crap, I'll keep thinking and not give you an answer today!" Sasha snapped back.

"No! No! Sasha my bad. Don't do that girl." Roxy said calmly.

"That's what I thought because you need me more than I need you Roxy!" Sasha snapped.

"Y-you right Sasha. So what you say? You gonna join the team?" Roxy asked. Sasha laughed and replied, "Yes Roxy."

"Thank you Sasha." Roxy said smiling.

"Wait chick! I got something else we got to agree on before I finalize anything." Sasha said seriously.

"Whatever you say I'll agree to, Sasha." Roxy

said before listening.

"Alright… so I want 75% of my money instead of 40." Sasha said.

"Wait up Sasha now you know—" Roxy tried to say.

Sasha interrupted.

"Stop right there before you finish Roxy. You just said *whatever* I say you'll agree with."

"But… but." Roxy stuttered.

"Naw, naw. I don't want to hear that crap. Roxy, you said what you meant so I'm getting 75% and you'll get 25% or I'll dance somewhere else!" Sasha said.

Roxy gave in and said, "Deal Sasha, okay?"

Sasha replied, "Alright, I'll start Monday night."

Roxy gladly said, "Okay good see you Monday night."

"Bye Roxy!" Sasha replied.

Roxy hung up and called Peezy.

Ring.

"I'm guessing you calling to tell me good news or you can hang up. Just tell me!" Peezy said.

"She said yes, Peezy." Roxy replied.

"Awe hell chick. I was ready to beat your ass!" Peezy said.

"But…" Roxy stumbled.

"What you do Roxy?" Peezy asked.

"Well, well I kinda told her she could get 75% and the club get 25%." Roxy replied slowly.

"Chick… why you do something like that?" Peezy asked.

"That's the only way she would join us Peezy. You said 'do what I had to do' to get her to say yes." Roxy pleaded.

"I didn't say be *dumb* Roxy. You should've threatened her if she didn't take your offer." Peezy said angrily.

"It's done now so what you want me to do?" Roxy replied.

"This time, and this time only, I'll let you get away with this dumb decision only because my club is booming and I'm just part owner in yours." Peezy said laughing. "Th—thank you Peezy." Roxy stuttered.

"Whatever. Get off my damn phone before I change my mind."

As Peezy hung up, Sugar called Roxy.

Ring…Ring…Ring.
"Hello!" Sugar said.

"What is it Sugar?" Roxy asked.

"When you opening your club?" Sugar asked.

"Ummm!" Roxy replied.

"What's wrong Roxy?" Sugar asked.

"Nothing, nothing. It opens Monday." Roxy stumbled.

"Can I work for you? I don't like it here anymore." Sugar pleaded.

"Umm Sugar? You at the best place. Why would you leave Peezy?" Roxy said.

"It's not the best place Roxy." Sugar replied.

"Sugar, I'll talk to you later okay." Roxy said.

"Fine!" Sugar yelled.

"Bye!" Roxy said and hung up.

Chapter 6

A Glimpse of The Past

❧

As friends, Layna and Sasha met at Layna's home to discuss the things going on in each of their lives. Sasha walked up to Layna's door and knocked on the door.

Knock! Knock!

"Sasha is that you?!" Layna asked.

"Yes, it's me," Sasha replied.

"Come on in girl," Layna said opening the door.

"Hey baby!" Sasha said hugging Layna.

"Hey Sasha! You okay girl?" Layna replied.

"Honestly, I'm okay. But I really need to just talk to you," Sasha said sadly.

"I'm always here to listen and help as I can. You know that," Layna said.

"Well Lay, as I made the decision to work for Roxy, it made me think about how before Roxy did her bid and my bad encounter as a young dancer," Sasha said with tears in her eyes.

"Keep talking Sha," Layna said.

"Well… you know Roxy is my mom's sister and she got me after mom passed. My life has been a roller coaster since," Layna said.

"I'm listening baby girl," Sasha continued.

"Before she went away, she had me do this huge drug encounter with her Plug which led to her making me become *his* girl so she could get her drugs for lower prices. I come to find out he also owned a strip club!"

Surprised Layna said, "Wait Sasha! So that's—"

Sasha stopped Layna and said, "Wait Layna, let me finish—come to the realization I was only 16—him 28 at the time. Roxy suggested I dance after school for a few hours. That's how I began dancing."

Shocked, Layna said, "Wow! Sasha… I had no idea the old chick was your aunt." Sasha replied, "Yes. She and I fell out after I started keeping my money instead of letting her take it. I worked hard for that money just to let her have it. So at 17, I ran away ending up with the plug."

"Dang Sasha!" Layna said in awe.

"Yes, it was bad. She ended up getting set up by the police a few days later. She thought that I had something to do with it, but in all honesty, I didn't." Sasha explained.

"So that's why she claims that you owe her?" Layna asked.

"Yes, but I really don't. That's why she will pay me 75% of my earnings instead of 45%," Sasha said smiling.

"Sasha how did you pull that off?" Layna asked.

"I didn't give her a chance to say no. She either let me get what I wanted or I walked!" Sasha said maliciously.

"Wow, I'm amazed! As hard as she claims to be, I'd think it'd be harder to get her to crack," Layna said.

"She is hard. I don't know why it was so easy, but I'm glad it was," Sasha replied. "Well, guess it was your lucky night," Layna said laughing.

"Maybe so, but she seemed scared so she may just have had to do whatever to get me to say yes," Sasha said thinking.

"Naw Sasha. She couldn't be scared you know? Roxy ain't scared of nobody," Layna replied.

"That may be right. Something's up though… I can feel it," Sasha said.

"Something good or bad Sha'?" Layna asked concerned.

"I don't know, but I'm going to find out." Sasha

replied.

"Sasha... I can't handle something happening to you again now." Layna said sadly.

"Ain't nothing gonna happen Lay. Calm down." Sasha replied.

"I hope that's true because somebody gonna get a bullet if it does," Layna said grabbing her gun.

"Girl, you always ready to shoot somebody!" Sasha said laughing.

"You damn right— over the people I love!" Layna said seriously.

"That gun gonna get you in trouble Lay!" Sasha replied seriously.

Layna smacked her lips and said, "No it ain't. It's gonna keep me out of it girl."

Laughing, Sasha said, "Let's talk about something else Lay— with your crazy self."

Layna said smiling, "What exactly do you want to talk about Sasha?"

"Anything besides me and my run-ins... and problems." Sasha replied.

"I don't have anything going on girl, so I guess we need to check the block and collect our money." Layna suggested.

"Right Lay. Knowing we need all that, will you do the pickups alone today?" Sasha asked.

"Yea I will, but why Sha?" Layna asked.

"I need to get some things together and check some things out." Sasha replied.

"I guess girl. I'll call you when I collect it all and we can count and split." Layna said.

"Alright girl. Love you." Sasha said walking to the door.

"Love you too Sha." Layna replied.

Sasha walked out of Layna's home and made a phone call to Peezy.

Ring. Ring.

Peezy picked up saying, "It's Peezy, who this?"

"Hey Peezy! This Sasha. I got some questions for you." Sasha replied.

"Alright shawty. What is it? You coming in or you asking over the phone?" Peezy asked.

"Over the phone if that's cool with you." Sasha replied.

"Already. Talk to me." Peezy said.

"You are part owner in Roxy's club ain't you?" Sasha asked.

"Yea Shawty." Peezy replied.

"What she got going on and why was it so easy for me to get what I wanted?" Sasha asked.

"Honestly, I don't know baby girl, but if I find something out I'll let you know." Peezy replied.

"Peezy, you know so tell me." Sasha snapped.

"Girl I said I don't, so stop asking me! I said I'll try to find out." Peezy snapped back.

"Yea, I hear you. Y'all bet not be on no 'foul stuff' or it's gonna be a war!" Sasha said maliciously.

"I don't do too well with threats shawty!" Peezy said angrily.

"It ain't a threat shawty. It's a promise!" Sasha snapped.

"Well ma'am, you got about five mo' minutes on my phone talking crap." Peezy replied.

"Girl I will ruin the whole business. Know that I'm two times a worse as Roxy claims to be!" Sasha threatened.

"Look shawty, your time is up and we done talking." Peezy said.

"Yea, alright. But know I'm forreal." Sasha replied.

"Aite!" Peezy said.

"Bye!" Sasha said as she made it to Roxy's club to get some things together for Monday night with it being Sunday night.

Ding Dong. Ding Dong.

The door rang as Sasha walked in. She could hear Roxy yelling on the phone.

"What are you talking about? I didn't tell

nobody to do that… hell nah. I—I don't know."

Sasha walked up and asked, "Who you talking to Roxy?"

Roxy jumped and said, "Sasha what you doing here?"

Sasha snapped, "Well for one, it's Sunday night and I start tomorrow. I need to set up."

"Oh, okay. Well let me get off this phone and I'll show you around." Roxy replied. "Alright Roxy!" Sasha said.

Roxy returned to the phone call and said, "C—can I call you back? But…okay bye!"

Walking toward the back Roxy said, "Come on Sasha, let's go to the back." "Following you!" Sasha said rolling her eyes.

"Right this way. You can go in here and pick anyone you want." Roxy said.

"Roxy, I want that room right there. That's a two-person room right!?" Sasha said. "Yea but…" Roxy said.

"Aunty, stop playing." Sasha said side-eyeing Roxy.

"You still claim me, Wok?" Roxy asked sadly.

"Yea, whatever Helena!" Sasha said.

Tears came to Roxy's eyes, but she quickly changed the subject and said, "Well Sha', go ahead and get the studio and I'll let you pick your partner in crime."

Sasha replied. "Okay, thanks Helena. I'll be back Monday night at 9 p.m."

"Okay, be careful out there." Roxy said.

"Aite, later." Sasha replied.

As Sasha walked out, she called Layna.

Ring. Ring.

"Hello?" Layna answered.

"Layna, you asleep?" Sasha asked.

"Girl, it's just 10:15 p.m." Layna replied.

"Well, you never know." Sasha said giggling.

"What's up baby girl?" Layna asked.

"I'm finna head over there." Sasha replied.

"Alright girl, come on." Layna said hanging up.

Chapter 7

Monday Night

Roxy and Peezy arrived at the club around 7:30 p.m. to get the building together. "Aye shawty, you know that little chick called me trying to check me right?" Peezy said angrily.

"Who Peezy?" Roxy asked.

"Sasha's punk ass!" Peezy yelled.

"Naw I didn't know? What did she say?" Roxy asked.

"Wanch talking about she'll ruin me and bull crap like that, but wait on it. I'm gonna get that chick later!" Peezy threatened.

"Wait now Peezy. I'm pretty sure whatever the disagreement was, it wasn't that serious." Roxy said calmly.

"I don't care Roxy! I got the chick's number. She gonna get it! I'm gonna give her plenty time to forget." Peezy said maliciously.

"Please Peezy, don't hurt her." Roxy pleaded.

"Shut up before I slap yo' ass!" Peezy said angrily.

Roxy walked off thinking what she had gotten her and Sasha into.

Sasha showed up and went to her dressing room to get ready. Roxy walked to her dressing room to see if she was ready.

Knock. Knock.
"Yo' who is it? Who is it?" Sasha asked.
"It's Roxy." Roxy replied.
"Come in Aunty," Sasha said.
"Hey Wok. I was just coming to see if you was ready you go on in 20 minutes." Roxy said as she walked in.
"Yea, I'm ready." Sasha replied.
"Alright. Stage six with the purple light is you baby." Roxy said softly.
"Yea, Helena. I'll be right out." Sasha replied.
As awkward as it may sound, Sasha said a quick prayer before her act.

The announcer said, "Coming to the stage... *Chocolate Delight!*" He shouted.
Like clockwork, Sasha got on the pole and worked her magic while the money flowed as she knew they would. As she was dancing, she saw one of her old customers walk up, so she went harder. As Sasha's dance ended, she greeted him.

"Hey Mr. LJ. How you been?"

"I've been great. Never thought I'd see you back in here." Mr. LJ replied.

"Me neither, but here I am." Sasha said smiling.

"I'm glad I got to see you in action again. Here's $200 for old times' sake." Mr. LJ said.

"Thank you, Mr. LJ. You were always my favorite. See you later." Sasha said hugging him.

"Bye darling," Mr. LJ replied.

Sasha walked to the bar to order food. Before she went back to her dressing room, Peezy just happened to walk up and say, "Hey chick!"

"Who!" replied Sasha.

"You the only chick I see standing here."

"Girl, bye! I'm talking to you girl!" Peezy said.

"Peezy, when you come correct we can 'conversate'. Until then, you talking to yourself. I gotta go count my money. Tell them to bring my food to Suite 11." Sasha said walking off.

Sasha got back to the dressing room and found Sugar.

"Who are you and why you in my dressing room?" Sasha asked with an attitude. "Hey, I'm Sugar. Roxy told me to come in here." Sugar replied.

"Alright, I guess you bet not be one of them thieving chicks. I'll whoop your ass." Sasha threatened.

"I don't steal and what's your name? I don't remember getting it." Layna said softly.

"My bad girl. My name is Sasha and they call me, *Chocolate Delight,*" Sasha said as she 'dropped it like it's hot'.

"Well, nice to meet you. Hopefully we become great friends." Layna said.

"Maybe so Sugar. I don't know... we will see." Sasha replied.

"It's my time to go on. Bye girl!" Sugar said.

"Alright, I'll be gone when you get back. Be safe." Sasha said nicely.

"Be careful getting out of here Sasha." Sugar said.

Sasha got her phone to call Roxy.

Ring. Ring. Ring.

"Hello." Sasha said.

"Hey Sasha! What's up?" Roxy replied.

"I got your money for the night. I'm finna head out." Sasha said.

"Alright baby, be safe. I'll see you Wednesday right?" Roxy asked.

"Yes, I'll be back." Sasha said laughing.

"Alright, bye honey." Roxy said.

"Bye Helena." Sasha said hanging up and leaving.

Chapter 8
Chill Day at Layna's

Sasha walked up to Layna's door.

Knock. Knock.

"Who is it?" Layna said. "It's me chick!" Sasha replied.

"Come in girl!" Layna said excited.

"Hey baby." Sasha greeted Layna.

"Hey my *chocolate* friend!" Layna yelled, sticking her tongue out.

"I missed you Lay!" Sasha yelled.

"I missed you too! How was your first night at the club?" Layna said.

"It was pretty girl. I made $5000, so I'd say it was successful!" Sasha said.

"Damn Sha', you made a grip." Layna said shocked.

"Yass girl. Told you that you should join me with all that sexiness girl. They would love you." Sasha said.

Layna interrupted, "—Don't mean to shut

you off, but girl… I'd never dance. It's just not something I'm interested in."

"Well girl, I'm trying to get rich by any means." Sasha replied.

"I've been thinking a lot Sha'. This fast money is good, but I think I'm finna call it quits soon." Layna said seriously.

"Layna, what's wrong?" Sasha asked.

"Nothing's wrong. I just don't want it to catch up with me at the wrong time." Layna replied.

"We ain't never got caught Lay. We too lowkey and so are our guys." Sasha said. Layna replied seriously, "Sasha, that doesn't mean it can't happen. I never want my future family to google me and find a mug shot."

Realizing what Layna was saying, Sasha said, "I see what you mean, but I'm not stopping no time soon."

Layna replied, "Okay girl!"

"Has J called you?" Sasha asked.

"Sasha, you know he's been worried about how your first night went." Layna said rolling her eyes.

"Why he be so worried about me?" Sasha asked with attitude.

"Girl, you know he been liking you for years now." Layna said looking at Sasha crazily.

"You know J is not my type. He not hard

enough for me." Sasha said smacking her lips.

"Girl... Sha' you crazy! What you want somebody who's gonna beat you half to death or something?" Layna asked a little annoyed.

"Naw Lay. It's not that. I just want... I don't know how to explain it." Sasha tried to explain.

"Whatever girl. Let it. Had it been me that J liked, I'd greatly accept all he's trying to give." Layna said.

"Well you should Lay. I don't want him." Sasha said.

"Sasha, I'm not doing that. One day you gonna come to your senses and love J." Layna said seriously.

"Girl you are crazy! Layna let's go get something to eat. I'm hungry." Sasha replied.

"Girl I wish you would go and get food! I cooked for us." Layna snapped.

"What you cook Lay-Lay?" Sasha asked smiling.

"Baked barbecue chicken, homemade white cheddar mac and cheese, greens, cornbread, and a small pot of pintos and ground beef just for you." Layna replied. "Owie! Layna girl I love you so much! You gonna make somebody a good wife one day!" Sasha said hugging Layna.

"I love you too *choc,* and I know girl. I'm going

to wait on God though. No rush." Layna replied.

"Well let's eat and talk girl," Sasha said walking to the kitchen.

"Okay, come on." Layna said getting the plates.

Chapter 9

Wednesday Night
A Night to Remember

Sasha ended up crashing at Layna's house after that great meal.

"Phew sis. I didn't even mean to go to sleep, but that food was so good. I got full and tapped." Sasha said smiling.

"It's okay Sha. I don't mind. You know you are always welcome here anytime." Layna said stretching.

"Thanks babe. I can always count on you. If nobody else got me, I know you do." Sasha replied still smiling.

"No thanks needed boo. That's what friends are for." Layna said.

"Right. Well I'm gonna run home and take a shower, get dressed, and ready for tonight." Sasha said walking to the door.

"Okay, but before you leave Sha', I want to pray

with you. With all the things that happened when you were first dancing, I don't want anything bad happening to you." Layna said gracefully.

"Okay Lay. I'm down for that." Sasha replied.

Grabbing Sasha's hands, Layna began, "Bow your head babe. Lord God, I'm coming to you as humble as I know how today. I'm coming to you asking if you could cover my friend with the blood as she goes to her job, God. We know that anything can happen and Lord I know that you can do all things. So Lord, please... *please* protect her from danger. Amen."

Hugging Layna, Sasha said, "Amen. Thank you, Layna. I love you girl. See you later."

In reply Layna said, "Okay. Love you too hun. I'll see you."

"Oh Lay. Be careful picking up the drops and the money. I hate that you are doing it alone." Sasha said concerned.

"Don't worry about me boo. I'll always be good. You just make sure you stay out of dangers way." Layna replied.

"I will, I will." Sasha said walking out.

For some reason, Layna just didn't feel right about this night, but she just didn't say anything.

8 p.m. came and Sasha arrived at the club to

prepare to get ready. She walked in and started walking to her dressing room when she saw Peezy.

"Aye, Aye!" Peezy yelled.

"What Peezy? I have to go get dressed!" Sasha snapped.

"Look, I don't need no attitude. I'm your boss too." Peezy said.

"Listen, if you have something to say, just say it and stop all the other talk." Sasha said rolling her eyes.

"Who the hell you think you talkin' to?" Peezy asked.

"See that's why you can't talk to me. I don't got time for you. Bye!" Sasha snapped.

Peezy mumbled under her breath, "Alright chick. Tonight's the night I'm gonna let you make me some money first though."

Roxy walked in Sasha's dressing room and said, "Hey Wok. You o—"

Sasha snapped, "Cut it Helena!"

Concerned, Roxy asked, "What's wrong baby?"

Sasha started talking, "For one, I'm tired of Peezy coming to me with that bull and talking crazy like I won't beat her ass in here."

Still worried Roxy asked, "Wait what she say to you?"

Sasha replied, "Just calling me out of my name and bumping up against me and crap. She better be glad I want to make this money tonight or I'd kick her ugly ass."

"It won't be none of that in here Wok. Just do what you have to do and leave. Don't worry about her." Roxy said hoping she listened.

Sasha replied, "Alright aunty." Walking to the door, Roxy said, "Oh yea and you on in about three minutes. Same stage, same color."

"Okay, I'll be right out." Sasha said and quickly said a prayer and went to the stage.

When Sasha got out there, she felt a little weird, but she started to dance anyway. The crowd was big tonight. They made her feel pretty good. Layna popped up and started throwing money yelling, "Go chocolate! Go chocolate! Get it girl!"

Smiling, Sasha climbed to the top of the pole and twerked all the way down to end her show.

"Layna, come here." Sasha said as she was picking up her money.

"Hey chick, meet me in the back in 30. I should be done counting and dressed by then."

"Love, I'll be waiting at my house finna check out these wings first."

"Okay girl." Sasha said. As Sasha walked back

to her suite, she saw Peezy and prayed she didn't say anything because all she wanted to do was count, leave their half, and leave.

"Hey chick, I need to talk to you." Peezy said.

Sasha replied, "Look Peezy, I'm tired. Can we talk tomorrow or something?"

"Nah chick. You gonna talk to me now." Peezy said maliciously.

"First off, I'm not talking to no damn body talking like that!" Sasha snapped. "Alright chick I tried." Peezy said as she drew her gun and shoots Sasha twice. ***BOOM! BOOM!***

She walked off saying, "Stupid chick."

Immediately Sugar ran out of the suite and found her and frantically started yelling, "Help! Help! Somebody help!"

Roxy ran out and yelled, "What is it Sugar!?"

Yelling, Sugar said, "Look Roxy!"

"Oh my God no!" Roxy yelled taking her phone out dialing 911.

"Yes, this is Helena Mcbee and I have a shot victim at my club. I need someone as soon as possible. Please! Please!" she yelled.

Calmly the dispatcher said, "Ma'am I need you to calm down and tell me the address."

Stuck, Roxy said, "Ummm!"

Again the dispatcher said, "Ma'am I need you

to tell me the address so I can send someone."

Snapping back into reality, Roxy said, "359 N. Kennedy Street!"

In reply the dispatcher said, "Okay ma'am. We will have someone there soon."

Eyes filled with tears, Roxy said, "Th—Thank you!"

Dropping to her knees Roxy began to hug Sasha as she slowly saw her drifting away.

So she began to pray, "Lord, I know I don't come to you often, but Lord please spare my niece. Lord… she is all I got and my sister left me over her. I've failed her Lord! Please… please… please don't let her leave! Amen."

Running in the EMT's yelled, "Where's the victim? Where's the victim?"

"Here she is" Roxy yelled.

Roxy didn't want to let her go as she told the EMT.

"Please do whatever you can to bring her back to me. Please… I need her."

In reply, he said, "We will do everything we can ma'am."

"Thank you. I'll be there soon baby," Roxy sadly told Sasha as she kissed her head.

The police came in to question everyone and Roxy was first.

"Ma'am can you step aside with me?" Officer James asked.

Roxy replied, "Yes… anything sir."

"Mrs. Mcbee, I'm going to ask you a few questions." Officer James said.

"Okay." Roxy replied.

"Where were you when the shooting took place?" James asked.

"I was in the office and I heard Sugar yelling for help. So, I ran out and saw Sasha shot on the floor." Roxy replied.

"Did you happen to see who shot her?" James questioned.

"No sir, but I have an idea who it was." Roxy said.

"Who Ma'am?" James asked.

"Peezy!" Roxy answered.

"Who is that and where is she/he?" James asked confused.

"It's a girl and I don't where she went, but can't you track her cellphone." Roxy said.

"Yes ma'am. Do you have her number?" James said.

"Yes, she has two: (543)983-3928 is her business and (948)392-0929 is the other." Roxy replied.

"Thank you, ma'am. We will be in touch." James said getting ready to leave.

"Thank you so much. I'd greatly appreciate that." Roxy said sadly.

Barely able to walk, Roxy made her way to Sasha and Sugar's dressing room to find Sugar laying on the floor crying.

Roxy grabbed Sugar and said, "Come here baby. I want to thank you for doing what you did. It took great bravery. Thank you."

In tears Sugar said, "You're welcome Mrs. Roxy. I'd want somebody to do it for me if I was on that floor."

Teary eyed, Roxy said, "Right baby. I—I'm just lost right now. She's my only blood."

Sugar replied, "I never knew she was kin to you Mrs. Roxy."

Roxy said, "Yes, she's my niece."

Sugar asked, "You going to the hospital?"

Sadly Roxy said, "Yes… finna go now. Had to come thank you for alerting me." Sugar replied, "Anytime Roxy. Be careful."

Roxy sadly said, "I will love. Get dressed, go home, and be careful too."

As Roxy was leaving, she called Layna.

Ring. Ring. Ring.

Layna answered, "Roxy, why you—."

Roxy yelled, "Wait Layna just listen!"

Calming down, Layna said, "Why you crying

Roxy?"

Roxy stumbled. "It's…it's…"

Confused Layna asked, "What Roxy?"

Crying, Roxy yelled, "Sasha got shot tonight!"

Angrily Layna asked, "What the hell you just say chick?"

Trying to calm down, Roxy said "Sasha got shot."

Livid, Layna said, "Who the hell did it? Somebody finna die today!"

Calmly Roxy said, "Layna, let the police handle it."

Pissed, Layna yelled, "Naw, damn! I knew when she was getting into messing with you somebody finna feel me!"

"Layna, I know you hurt. I am too, but let them handle it… please." Roxy pleaded. "Get off my damn phone Roxy!" Layna yelled.

"Layna, don't you want to know where she is?" Roxy asked.

"Yes chick!" Layna yelled.

"She's at St. Peters." Roxy calmly said.

"Yea!" Layna yelled and hung up.

Click!

Chapter 10
The Hospital

❦

As Roxy walked in the hospital, she was completely lost so she walked up to the desk and the nurse greeted her.

"Hello ma'am, how can I assist you?"

Roxy replied, "Um… I'm looking for my niece, Sasha McFarely."

Smiling the nurse said, "Oh ma'am, I've been waiting on someone for Mrs. McFarely. Are you close to kin?"

Roxy responded, "Yes ma'am, I'm her aunt."

The nurse said, "Ma'am, I have good and bad news. The good news is she went through surgery well and the bullet was removed. Because of so much blood loss and two blood transfusions, she slipped into a coma."

Roxy yelled, "No! I can't lose her! Why!?"

Trying to calm Roxy down, the nurse grabbed her and said, "Mrs. Mcbee, I know you're hurting, but I want to encourage you that this doesn't mean death. With strong faith, you can pray her out of that coma. God can do anything if you believe."

Tears falling, Roxy asked, "Baby what's your name?"

"Nika ma'am." Nika answered.

"Well Nika baby, I'm sure God doesn't want to hear from me," Roxy said sadly. "Why do you say that Mrs. Mcbee?" Nika asked.

"A sinner like me… I'm sure my prayer wouldn't get through." Roxy replied.

"Just try it for yourself ma'am. It will work. Just believe." Nika said.

"I'll try it. Hopefully it will work." Roxy said.

"Believe! Just believe." Nika encouraged.

"Okay baby, okay." Roxy replied rolling her eyes.

"I'll be praying for her daily." Nika promised.

"I really thank you darling. She's going to need it. What room is she in?" Roxy asked.

"445 N— to your left." Nika directed.

Roxy walked off to the room slowly breaking down at the thought of losing Sasha and it being her fault made her want to lose life herself. Roxy built up the courage to walk in the room to find Plug J and Layna.

Layna couldn't keep her composure with tears

falling down her face and words barely noticeable as she talked to Sasha.

"Sasha, please don't leave me here alone. You are the only person that truly looks out for me. What am I going to do Sha'? Please talk to me. I just want to hear you tell me you okay!"

J grabbed and hugged her, and said with tears in his eyes, "Shawty, I'm gonna help you get through this. I'll be here every day until whatever happens… happens, and best believe I got somebody looking for the person that did this. They better hope 50 get to them before they do."

Layna replied crying, "Thank you J. I know you really love Sha'. Man, we gotta pray her out of this!"

"Shawty… honestly I don't know how to pray, but if it will help Sasha, I'm going to try it out." J said.

"I'll help you. I've been building a better relationship with the man above." Layna replied.

As Roxy tried to ease the door up, J heard it and immediately said, "Aye who is it?"

Roxy said nothing and walked around the corner.

Layna looked and said, "I knew it was you. As bad as I want to get at you for Sasha's sake, I'm gonna let you live this time even though th—."

"Wait!" Roxy said.

"Wait for what? This is your fault." Layna snapped.

Roxy broke down with tears flowing and said, "Layna, I feel bad enough. My sister asked me to keep her safe with her last breath, and yet I've put her through hell and hot water. Now I got to live with the fact that she may die and it be because of me. I've not only failed my sister, but my niece too! That ain't a good feeling Layna I feel the same pain you feel. She all I got out here too."

Layna said hysterically, "Why did you even come back in her life? She was doing great without you man!"

Sadly, Roxy replied, "I don't even have a good answer to that. I wish I would've stayed away."

J stepped in between the two and said, "Instead of us talking about what could've been— if we'd done this or that, let's focus on Sasha and her getting well. This negativity… she feels it and she don't need it around her."

"Aite J." Layna said.

"You're right son." Roxy said.

"Aye Lay, if you need me hit my line imma bounce. I'll be back tomorrow."

Layna and J hugged and said their goodbyes.

Layna kissed Sasha on the forehead and

said, "Baby, I'll be here every day until you pull through. I know God will bring you through this. I love you baby girl."

Alone with Sasha, all Roxy could do was cry because she knew no words to say. Nika walked in and said, "Mrs. Mcbee."

Teary-eyed, Roxy looked up and said, "Yes."

"May I pray with you if you don't mind?" Nika asked.

"If it will help Sasha, yes." Roxy sadly replied.

"Okay. Will you hold mine and Sasha's hand?" Nika asked.

"Yes" she replied.

Nika put her hand on Sasha's stomach and began to pray heavily.

"Lord, today I lift Sasha's young body to you asking that you show up in her life and change her circumstance as she is absent from the body. Lord, let her experience your presence. Save her soul. Lord, bless her family members and friends to know that you're a doctor that can heal anyone if they just believe in this time. Lord, make their walks closer to you for they may be blind and don't truly know who you are. Make a believer out of them Lord God and make your presence known as I'm praying now. Lord, touch

Mrs. Mcbee's heart and lighten her load for the burden of losing her niece is taking all life out of her right now. In your darling son Jesus' name I pray, Amen."

"Amen." Roxy said as she got up to hug Nika's neck.

"Thank you, baby."

"It's my great pleasure ma'am. I became a nurse to save lives and that's what I'm going to do. I'm going to come pray with Sasha every day that I am at work if that's okay." Nika replied.

"Of course, baby. Please do." Roxy said.

Roxy sat and held Sasha's hand and finally words came to her.

"Wok, I'm so sorry for everything I put you through. I failed you greatly and I'll never forgive myself for it because your ma' had faith in me to finish raising you. As good as she did, I didn't want to tell her. I didn't know how to do the task that she left for me, so I just said yea. When I knew that the streets was all I knew and I had no time for a teenager, I could barely keep up with myself. I just didn't want to let her down for she asked me before she took her last few breaths."

Crying heavily now, Roxy continued, "Baby, I should've never put you in the game or let that dirty grimy fool do the things he done to you.

If I could take it all back, I would. I love you so much. I can't stand to see you like this because of me— because of *me*... oh why couldn't it be me instead of you? I'm the one who really deserved a bullet— ME!"

As morning came, Roxy realized that she had cried herself to sleep while holding Sasha's hand. "Baby, I'll be back. Please don't leave me." Roxy said as she kissed her jaw and walked out.

Nika greeted Roxy, "Hello Mrs. Mcbee. Have a blessed day! See you soon."

"Hey baby, thank you." she replied walking lifelessly out of the door.

Day in and day out Roxy, Plug J, and Layna visited Sasha and talked to her. Meanwhile, Nika went into the room and prayed five times a shift for Sasha.

Chapter 11
The Experience

While Sasha Lay in her coma, she experienced God up close and personal. Sasha saw a bright light and a man walking toward her.

He approached her and said, "My child, I have a few propositions for you. Are you ready?"

"Yes sir" Sasha replied.

"First, I'll let you see your mom briefly. Cherish the moment," said the Lord. "Thank you, Lord," Sasha said gratefully.

"Hello love," Lona said as she came in.

"Mama... is it really you?" Sasha asked.

"Yes baby." Lona replied.

"Mama— oh how I miss you. I've been dreaming of the day that I got to talk to you again. I never said goodbye because I didn't want to let you go." Sasha said grabbing her mom tightly.

"Baby, I'm happy to see you again too. I love you and I watch you daily." Lona replied.

"I love you to Mama." Sasha said still holding on.

"Come my child," said the Lord.

Crying, Sasha pleaded, "No! Please, can I have a few more minutes?"

Lona told Sasha, "Baby, go. Momma loves you."

Sadly, Sasha replied, "Love you…"

"My child, I'm going to give you the opportunity to have a second chance if you make me one promise," said the Lord."

In reply Sasha said, "Lord… whatever you ask me, I'll do."

"When I bless you to go back, I ask of you to clean up your life completely. Give your life fully to me and spread my word. Save the lives of people like you starting with the people dear to you and share your testimony."

Thus said the Lord.

"I'll do it God!" Sasha replied.

"If you fail to live up to your promise, I shall take the breath from you and give you no more chances," God said.

Sasha gratefully said, "I won't fail you Lord. I thank you for giving me a chance to know that my mom is okay and looking over me."

God replied, "You're welcome my child. Now go fulfill my destiny for you."

As the light disappeared, Sasha said, "Yes Lord."

Chapter 12
The Last Prayer

As usual, Nika entered the room for the last time and began to pray.

"Lord God, I ask of you to bless Sasha to come out of this coma God, for I know that there is more that she has to accomplish before she leaves this earth. Lord, there are people who need just one more chance to love her and get things right. In your name I pray, amen."

Before Nika could open her eyes, she heard Sasha gasp for air and she immediately opened her eyes and said, "Sasha!"

Sasha looked around and said, "Where am I?"

Nika replied, "Love, you're in the hospital. You were shot and in a coma for five months! Your loved ones just left. I'm going to call them back. Will you be alright until I come back?"

Sasha said, "Yes, could you call Layna first please?"

Nika replied smiling, "Yes ma'am! Will do."

Sasha said gratefully, "Thank you!"

Nika ran to the desk and dialed Layna's number. By now Nika knew them personally.

Tap... tap... tap... tap... tap. Ring. Ring. Ring.

Nika said excitedly, "Layna, please come back to the hospital and tell J to come with you!"

Concerned, Layna said, "Okay Nika, but is everything okay?"

Nika replied— not wanting to tell the good news, "Just come Layna."

"Okay... headed that way."

As soon as Layna got off the phone, she called J.

Ring. Ring. Ring.

"Aye, what's up Lay?" J answered.

"J, come get me. Nika said come to the hospital." Layna said sadly.

"Is everything okay shawty?" J asked.

"I don't know J. Lets just get there!" Layna said hysterically.

"Around the corner. Come on," J said.

Layna ran out the door and waited until J pulled up.

Beep. Beep.

Layna waved J to come on and she jumped in.

"Hey, let's get there quick. I don't know what's

wrong, but I want to get there." Layna said worriedly.

"Buckle up shawty. We gonna get there," J said.

"J, what you think is wrong? You don't think Sha' died, do you? Oh my gosh J! I can't lose her!" Layna said crying.

"Lay-Lay calm down! Don't think the worst. Let's just get there and see okay?" With tears in his eyes, J just grabbed Lays hand.

"J, it's hard when the person you've seen go through so much that will do anything for anybody gets hurt like that. Yea man… she can be mean, but her heart is pure man."

J said sadly, "I know shawty. I know."

Layna asked, "J, will you pray with me?"

"I don't know how to start shawty. I do want to get closer to the man above though," J replied.

"I'll pray J." Layna said.

"Aite love." J replied.

J pulled up to the hospital and parked.

"What am I supposed to do Lay?" J asked.

"Close your eyes, bow your head, and hold my hands." Layna instructed.

"Okay." J replied.

Lay began to pray, "Lord, I'm coming to you the best way I know how. Please keep our minds open to whatever news is coming to us when we walk in this hospital. God, please... please Lord! Save my best friend. Please Lord... please. To get her back Lord, I'll quit the game today and give my life fully to you to have my best friend back. Bless her soul God. Help us to understand your will. Amen." "Amen," said J.

"You ready to go in J?" Layna asked.

"Yea shawty." J replied.

Lay took a deep breath and walked through the door to see Nika smiling.

"What is it Nika?" Layna asked.

"Go to the room Layna!" Nika replied.

Layna grabbed J's hand and walked in the room.

Sasha said, "Lay... is that you?"

Lay screamed, "Sasha!!" broke down crying and ran to the bed.

"I love you Sha'!"

Layna fell down on her knees, raised her hands and said, "Lord, I surrender! I'm giving my whole life to you. Use me in whatever way you would like. Thank you for sending my best friend back to me!"

"Amen," said Sasha.

Lay got up, hugged Sasha and said, "The thought of almost losing you opened my eyes so much Sha'. I'm done with the game— completely done. J, I'm sorry. I know this may upset you, but I can't do it no more. These streets are getting too dangerous for me. I want a future."

J replied, "Shawty, honestly I'm finna shut down the business and start a family myself, if Sasha will let me."

Layna and Sasha turned around. J was holding a ring, on one knee and said, "Sasha, I've had my eyes on you for some time now and to see you lay in that bed for five months 2 days 12 hours 15 mins and 39 seconds, I felt pieces of my heart breaking at the thought of never being able to have a chance to be with you. I came in here every day three times a day hoping that when you opened your eyes, I'd be the first person you'd see. It didn't happen that way, but I'm glad they opened. You getting shot made my cold heart pump warm blood again. You made my wall that I had built crumble to the ground and open up to love again. Will you please let me show you what love is? Please?"

Layna moved and let J get off his knee to come stand by the bed. Sasha with tears flowing looked up at J and said, "Yes! Promise me one thing…"

J replied, "Anything! What is it?"

Looking into his eyes, Sasha said, "You have to promise me you will get to know the real me and become my best friend, but most importantly… build a relationship with God and with me."

"I promise. I'll get to know every detail about you and be the superman you've always dreamed of having. Anytime you're down, I'm going to pick up the pieces and put them back together. I'm right now in this room giving my life fully to God. I'm going to give everything I have stored up back to the supplier and not getting any more. I'm going to apply for some jobs tomorrow. I have enough money saved up for 5 years," J replied.

Sasha grabbed J, kissed him and said, "I love you already!"

Smiling, J said, "I love you too *chocolate* girl!"

Layna just sat back and cried tears of joy.

She hugged them both and said, "I love y'all!"

Both replied, "We love you too Lay!"

Nika finally came in and said, "Hey guys! I wanted to give y'all some time together. I knew this moment would mean a lot to y'all. How's everyone doing?" Layna grabbed Nika, hugged her and said, "I want to thank you so much for praying with Sasha from day one. You saved her life Nika."

Nika stopped her and said, "I don't mean to interrupt you love, but that was all God. I was just doing what I knew best to do, and that's pray and believe in what I prayed. Look how God moved! I knew she wasn't leaving this soon. God just needed to talk to her about some things. I've grown to love y'all just as I do my family. Please promise that we'll stay connected."

Sasha replied, "We will because I need you to be a bridesmaid."

Nika looked and said, "Huh?"

Smiling, Sasha said, "J and I are getting married! He proposed a while ago."

Eyes filled with tears, Nika said, "My God my God! I'm so excited because I knew he loved you. That young man was here three— sometimes four times a day rubbing your hand, brushing your hair, and everything!"

J smiled and Sasha looked and said, "You did J?"

J replied, "Yea Sasha. Man, I really love you and if you would've said no, I would've still stuck around, helped nurse you back to health, and keep check on you."

Crying, Sasha said, "J, I don't know what to say. I'm just ready to start life with you!"

Nika began to talk.

"Well Sasha, I really came in to tell you that whenever you're ready, we can begin your therapy to get you back to walking and using that right arm."

"Will I do it here Nika?" Sasha asked.

"Yea." Nika tried to say.

J stopped her before she could begin and said, "No you won't baby because I'm taking you home. I'll be paying Nika and whatever else she needs to come to our home to take care of you until you're well again."

"J… really?" Nika asked.

"Of course, Nika! I'll pay you whatever. When can you start and what equipment do I need for her to start?"

Nika replied, "We just need some weights to strengthen her arm and just some rails and a hallway for her walking."

J said, "Consider it done! I have a few friends that can get me all that shawty. When can you start?"

Nika replied, "I have to talk to my boss to see if he can work with my schedule."

J stopped her and said, "Shawty, quit this job. I'll pay for whatever you need until my baby is well again and I'll make sure you get another job when she good again."

Surprised, Nika said, "You would do that?"

J replied, "Of course I will! You family now."

Nika said, "Thank you, and oh! Would you like

me to call Roxy??"

"Nah!" J said.

Sasha grabbed his hand and said, "Love, don't act like that. I have a few things to say to her. Let her come."

"She's the one that got you in this in the beginning Sha'!" Layna said angrily. Sasha said, "I love you both, but the Lord put some things on my heart to tell Roxy and I will do just as He instructed me, okay?"

Layna replied, "Okay Sasha."

"If that's what you want love, I'm behind you," J said.

"Nika, will you call her please?" Sasha asked.

"Yes Sasha! I'm on it," Nika replied.

Nika walked out the room and called Roxy.

Tap. Tap. Tap. Tap. Ring. Ring. Ring.

"Hello Roxy. This is Nika. Could you come to the hospital?" Nika said.

"Yes! Did something happen to Sha'?" Roxy replied.

"No ma'am, she actually woke up and would like to talk to you." Nika said. "Alright, tell her I'm on my way!" Roxy said.

"Yes ma'am! See you soon," Nika replied and hung up.

She walked back in the room. Sasha was talking to Layna and J.

"Y'all, it's time for us to give up all the street stuff and get our lives right with God. There are so many opportunities that could come to us if we just open the door and let God move for us. During my coma, it should've opened your eyes to know that death could happen at any second without warning. If you don't have it right, the devil won and you'll never get the chance to see those you love again. Like… my mom before she died always gave her all to God and she's resting eternally in his arms with no worries or cares of the world. When I die, I want to join her. It's amazing how God can move. He truly gave me a second chance and Nika's prayers brought Him to me clearly. Nika… I really thank you for the faith that you have that helped God come in and save me."

Nika replied, "You're welcome love. That's all I know to do in the time of trouble and that's seek His face and let Him fight all battles. I truly think that God put me in this position as a nurse because He knew I'd pray for all my patients when doctors have thought to give up. The power of prayer can save any life if you let Him and I'd love to help y'all get as close as I am to God."

"We'd love that," Sasha said.

"When you come to help nurse Sasha back to health, we all gonna help each other get closer to God. It's only right," J said.

"I'd love that," said Layna.

"I love y'all!" Sasha said. "We love you too Sasha," everyone said.

Roxy came in and said, "Sha' I'm so glad that you are doing good. I thought I was going to lose you."

Layna said angrily, "You better be glad we didn't lose her because I was gonna send you with her!"

"Layna, no! Stop that!" Sasha pleaded.

"I'm sorry Sasha. I'm only telling the truth. If you never started back dealing with her, this would've never happened in the first place!" Layna snapped.

"Layna, y'all step out while I talk to my aunt please." Sasha asked.

"Okay Sasha," Layna said.

Sasha grabbed J to stay. "You sure?" he asked.

"Yes please." Sasha replied.

"Anything you ask baby." J said.

"Can you raise my bed up a little for me J?" Sasha asked.

"Yes love," J replied.

"Thank you," Sasha said smiling.

"Roxy, come sit on the other side of me please. I want to look you in your eyes while I talk to you," Sasha said.

"Okay baby," Roxy answered.

"You probably think I blame you for what happened, but in all honesty, I'm grateful that it happened because while I was in that coma, I saw mama and she told me that she's not blaming you either. She wishes that you would've taken care of me better, but we can't take time back and I forgive you for all the hurt and pain you caused me. I don't hold a grudge aunty. There are some things you have to get right with yourself or you're going to be in the same situation. I'm in, but it's not going to end as well as I did. So I'm begging you get it right with God, dodge the bullet, and save yourself. I wouldn't be telling you this if God hadn't spoken it to me. You can think I'm crazy if you'd like. It's the God's honest truth." Sasha stressed.

With tears flowing down her face, Roxy said, "Niecy as you was talking to me, I felt chills run down my body the whole time and I know that could be nobody but God. I don't know how or where to start, but I want to experience God as you have and get my life together. I'm too old to be acting and doing the things I am. Will you please help me?"

Sasha replied, "Yes, I'll help you auntie. I want to see you better."

Gratefully Roxy said, "Thank you so much baby. My soul has been lost for a very long time and I let the darkness set in. I became very comfortable with how my life was going when all along, all I had to do was let God in. I could've had so many

blessings, but I missed them for fast money and a jail sentence."

Smiling, Sasha said, "Yes, that's exactly what you did, but those blessings can still happen. Nothing is too hard for God and the word says: 'If God is with you, who can stand against you?' Let Him move some mountains and make things shake for you. It just takes patience and believing in prayer."

Nika walked in and said, "Well Sasha, I have your discharge papers for you to sign and don't worry about any hospital bills. Everything has been paid in full."

Sasha looked at J.

J said, "Nah baby, wasn't me. I planned on it though." Sasha looked up and said, "Thank you Lord!"

J said, "So Nika, are you going to be our

full-time nurse? I'll pay you whatever they paid you— no taxes."

Gratefully Nika said, "Yes! I talked to my supervisor today. He said whenever I got her back to good health, I can have my job back with a raise."

"Look how good God is!" Sasha said.

"Right love. I was convinced that he would be very angry, but God!" Nika replied. "Yes!" Sasha said.

"I'll go turn these papers in and get a wheelchair for you," Nika said.

"Okay, thank you Nika!" Sasha replied.

"Baby, I'll be right back. Finna pull the truck around to the door. Tell Nika I'm going to put you in the chair." J said.

"Thank you J," Sash replied and began talking to Roxy.

"Auntie, when I get settled, I'll send you the address so you can come visit. Make sure you find you a bible and start reading the word and learning how to pray. If you need anything, call me. I'll be glad to help you."

Roxy replied, "I love you niecy!"

Smiling, Sasha said, "I love you too! Be careful in these streets, okay?"

Hugging Sasha, Roxy said, "I will love and I just

wanted you to know that they found Peezy. She is serving 15 years for attempted murder with no bail."

Sasha replied, "Okay auntie."

"See you later baby. Pray for me." Roxy pleaded.

"I will everyday auntie." Sasha said smiling.

"Okay love, I'm back. You ready to go?" Nika said rolling the wheelchair in. Sasha replied, "I'll wait for J to come back, but can I ask you something Nika?" "Yes of course love." Nika said.

"What brought you to God?" Sasha asked.

"Life and it's daily struggles. Honestly, I've been through a lot. I was pimped out against my will at a young age by my mom and her boyfriend. In my senior year of high school, they said it was to get me ready for the future. All and all, it hurt so much because I knew what I was going through, but I honestly wanted to save my virginity for marriage. My mother took that away just to get a few bucks. I've been pregnant four times and guess what? She made me have each one, so guess who had to struggle not knowing which man was the daddy or even what any of their names were— just faces in the dark now. I have to one day tell my babies why their dads have never been around and why they all look different. That made me turn over to God at twenty. When

I finally got away from my mom, her horrible drug habits, and her boyfriend, it's been up from then— blessings after blessings. That's why every time someone comes in, I pray for them. Rather small or big, God is a healer of all and that's why He sent me here."

Amazed Sasha said, "Wow! By looking at you I'd never know that you had four kids or been through all those things. I admire you for the way God has moved in you." Nika replied.

"Thanks love."

"You ready baby girl?" J walked in and asked.

"Yes love." Sasha answered.

As he picked her up, he whispered, "Thank you for saying yes to being mine forever."

Sasha replied, "Thanks for choosing me to be that girl."

"Nika, can you start tomorrow? I'm going to move you and your kids out that hood you in and you gonna move in the house down the street from us. I'm not taking no for an answer because I already paid for it and paid the bills up for three months." J said.

"Glory to God! I'm really at a loss for words right now. Thank you so much for everything! It means so much to me. I can't thank nobody but God for bringing you guys into my life making all these things possible. Is it okay if I hug you guys?" Nika said crying.

"Of course! That's fine love. You family now." Sasha said.

"Thank you so much." Nika replied as tears flowed down her.

Nika held Sasha so tightly.

"I'll have Sasha text you the address to your new home and you send her your old one. I'll send the movers to get your stuff to the new house and I put boxes in your car." J told Nika.

Grateful Nika said, "Thanks again… from the bottom of my heart."

"Fasho' shawty!" J replied.

Chapter 13

The Recovery

As Sasha and J walked in, Sasha said, "J, lets bless this house with prayer."

He replied, "Whatever you want to do baby, we will do."

In the living room, Sasha began to pray.

"Lord, today cover our home with your precious blood so that anytime that someone comes in our home, they feel your presence. Lord, bless me to be able to spread your goodness. Give me and J the wisdom that we lack. Lord, during this journey to recovery, give me the courage not to quit. We humbly give ourselves to you today Lord. Forgive us of our past sins. Guide us to bring our loved ones to you as we bring ourselves closer. In your name we pray, Amen."

J said, "Amen! Baby, that was beautiful. I'm so ready to become a better person so that when we decide to have children, we will have the tools to train them up right."

In reply Sasha said, "That's right baby, I love this house. I can't wait until I can move around and decorate."

Kissing Sasha J said, "I'm glad you like it. You deserve it all and I plan to give it to you."

Smiling, Sasha said, "Thank you J."

Smiling and grabbing her hand he said, "No thanks needed. Have you talked to Nika yet?"

Sasha replied, "Yes. I meant to tell you that she said the movers brought their things over and they are almost finished unpacking."

Nodding his head, J said, "Good. Did she say how long it was going to take to get you back right?"

Sasha replied, "She actually said it wasn't going to take long at all because the bullet didn't mess up anything. My legs just have to get back used to moving because I didn't use them for five months."

"So about two weeks?" J asked.

"Maybe not even that long. Shouldn't take long to get my strength back with prayer and believing in what I pray. God can make anything possible, that's why we have to get in our Bibles and start praying daily." Sasha said seriously. "Whenever you're ready baby, I'm ready." J replied.

"Not trying to be funny, but do you have any

bibles here?" Sasha asked.

"No shawty, but we can download some on our phones." J replied.

"You're right! Let's do that and while they are downloading, we can pray for our relationship." Sasha said softly.

"Okay love." J replied.

Sasha began to pray, "Lord, once again today I'm coming to you for strength and a better understanding of your will for us. Lord, give us your eyes so that we see all the things you want us to see clearly. Give us your heart so that we can give the love that you give. Change our minds to think as you'd like us to Lord. Before we walk down the aisle Lord, anoint us from the soles of our feet to the crown of our heads so that when trouble arises, we will be able to seek you and get back on the straight and narrow. God… even though the doctors said it will take two months before I walk again, I know that you are the head doctor and with you anything is possible. Heal my legs with your precious blood Lord God and show how quick you can work. Lord God, fill me with your presence so that I can share your word everywhere I step foot. In your name I pray, amen."

Shocked by the experience, J said, "Amen!

Baby... I felt chills the whole time you was praying. I know that only God could make that happen. I'm honestly ready to fully just let God in and live a good life. I've had so many dark days that I never want to see again and I know with God the dark days won't last long at all."

Sasha assured J, "You're right J. I'm going to make sure you do just that because God has so much in store for us if we just stay in Him *for* Him always."

"We will Sha." J promised.

"I'm really tired. Could you lay me down please?" Sasha said softly.

"Yes." J replied.

"Thanks baby." Sasha said.

"You're welcome. You have a long day ahead of you tomorrow. Get your rest. I love you." J said lovingly.

"I love you too J." Sasha replied laying down.

As they laid, J rubbed Sasha's hair and silently prayed.

"Lord although I don't know how to pray properly, I'm seeking you for healing for Sasha's legs. Bless her to walk soon so that she can begin to pursue her dreams. Help me to be the man of God that she needs me to be. Forgive me of all my sins. Please God... I know I've done many bad things and I regret them all. Help me not to ever be that guy again! Mold me to be just the man that you were here on earth. Cleanse my body of all imperfections please. Lord thank you for listening and amen."

Feeling at peace, J laid down, held Sasha, and fell asleep.

Knock. Knock. Knock.

"Baby! Baby!" Sasha yelled.

"You okay Shay?" J ran and asked.

"Yes, I'm okay. Someone's at the door." Sasha replied.

"Oh okay. I'll go check it out." J said in relief.

"Who is it?" J asked.

"It's Nika." Nika answered.

"Alright shawty, come on in." J said.

"Hey J! How are you today?" Nika said, greeting J.

"I'm good. You straight?" J replied.

"Yes, I'm fine. Do you need help dressing Sasha?" Nika said.

"Nah. I'll see if she wants you to come in while I'm changing her." J replied. "Who was it J?" Sasha asked.

"Nika's here to start your therapy. Do you want her to come in while I put your clothes on." J replied.

"That's fine, but I'd like to put them on and if I need your assistance, I'll ask. I don't want to become dependent on you guys." Sasha said.

"Okay. Let me tell Nika she can come in." J replied.

"Okay." Sasha said.

"Nika, come on in." J told Nika.

"Alright." Nika said as she walked in.

"Could you pick her clothes out? I'm not good with all that." J asked.

"Sure J." Nika said.

"Thank you." J replied.

"Hey beautiful girl! How are you feeling today?" Nika said smiling.

"I'm feeling blessed love! How are you?" Sasha said.

"I'm blessed and highly favored hun." Nika replied.

"There's no other way to be Nika." Sasha said.

"Right. Do you need help with those pants I see that you almost got them pulled up past your knees." Nika said.

"Could you pull them up over my feet and help me stand to pull them up?" Sasha asked.

"We surely can try that if you'd like." Nika said.

"Thank y'all so much for not telling me to wait.

I'm moving too fast because that's what I was looking for y'all to say." Sasha said gratefully.

"We are here to motivate and push you not hold you back." Nika said.

"Baby, I'll Hold your waist while you try." J said softly.

Sasha smiled, "Thank you J."

J replied, "Welcome love."

Sasha said excitedly, "Yes I did it!"

"Congratulations!" they both said.

"Nika… my legs just feel tingly like they are just asleep. I don't think it will take long." Sasha said.

"We are going to make sure of that because every day I come, we are going to pray over your legs. God's going to heal you quickly as long as you believe and trust in the power of prayer." Nika said.

"I promise I'll never doubt what the Lord will do for me. My faith is renewed and so am I." Sasha said.

Nika replied, "Great! Let's begin. Lord God, today I lift up Sasha's legs to you. Heal her quickly so that others can see how powerful you are and how fast you can move Lord. Give the abilities of her lower limbs so she can spread the goodness of gaining and keeping a relationship with you oh God, for you healed the woman with the issue of blood instantly because of how strong her faith was. So today Lord, we touch your cloak at this moment for healing. Lord, we thank you in advance for what you are about to do with our lives. In your great name we pray, amen."

Sasha put her right hand up and said, "Amen, thank you Lord."

Nika said, "Alright love, let's get started. Would you like me to wheel you to the rails or try to walk with J behind us with the chair— just in case you get weak." Smiling Sasha said, "I'd like to try to walk to them. Can J hold me though?"

Not surprised Nika said, "Of course he can! It's whatever you want love."

Sasha yelled, "Baby!!"

Running J said, "What's wrong baby?"

Sasha asked, "Can you help me walk to the rails?"

Calming down J said, "Yes baby. You really had me thinking you had gotten hurt or something."

In reply Sasha said, "I'm sorry, didn't mean to. Just wanted to get your attention." Kissing her forehead, he said, "It's fine love. Just glad you're okay. You ready?" "Yes." Sasha said.

"How do I hold her Nika?" J asked clueless.

"You could do three things. You could hold

her hands and walk backwards. She could use the walker, or lastly you could hold her waist and walk behind her." Nika explained.

"Which one you want to do baby?" J asked.

"I'll start with the walker. I have a little pain in my back." Sasha replied.

"That's what I figured. Take your time don't try to do too much." Nika said.

"Let's go love. Take your time." J said.

Sasha grabbed the walker and began to walk. She began to speak to God, "Lord, I'm weak. Make me strong and most importantly Lord thank you for it all. Thank you for this second chance on life. We all know I didn't deserve it with the path I was walking. I was lost and you found me and gave me grace and mercy. Thank you dear Lord! I'll forever be grateful for what you have done for me. In your name I pray, amen."

J said amazed, "That was beautiful baby! Do you want to rest for a little bit? You're close, but I don't want you hurting though."

Sasha said, "I'm okay love. God got me."

As God whispered to her, *"I got you."*

Amazed Nika said, "You're doing very well Sasha! I'm very proud of your fight and endurance. It takes a strong individual to do what you are doing." Nika said surprised at Sasha's progress.

"Honestly Nika, I'm ready to get back to me so that I can start spreading the word of God." Sasha said gracefully.

"Amazing! Love, you made it. We are going to do ten minutes walking on the rail, five minutes on the pedals, and we will see how long you can go to strengthen your back." Nika said.

"Okay, I'm ready. Baby, can I use your shoulder to get to the rails?"

J replied, "Of course! Whenever you're ready and then I'm going to go cook." Nika said, "J... start her out on like some chicken noodle soup because her stomach may be a little weak after those many months."

Sasha replied, "I've ate solid foods already Nika—not greasy, but J baked some chicken and did sweet potatoes and it went well."

"Oh okay. I figured that you'd get sick." Nika said shocked.

Sasha said smiling, "When God carries you, sickness doesn't last long and J can you go to the book store and pick up us some guides to 'stronger prayer life' and 'faith strengthening' books please?"

J replied, "Yes, I'll go real quick."

Enlightened by Sasha's wisdom, Nika said, "You're so right. Keep that frame of mind. It will take you very far in life. Keep letting him lead you."

Sasha said smiling, "I am. I promise you that."

Nika said smiling, "I'm proud of you Sasha!"

Sasha replied, "Thank you Nika!"

J walked in and said, "Baby, the food is ready. Are y'all almost finished? I got the books."

Sasha replied, "Yes— finishing up my back."

"Okay... are you going to eat before you shower?" J asked.

"Yes. What did you cook?" Sasha asked.

"White chicken, chili, and cornbread." J replied.

Sasha said gratefully, "Sounds delicious baby! Thank you."

J replied, "Welcome love. Nika I made a pot for you to take with you also." Overwhelmed, Nika said, "Thanks so much. I greatly appreciate y'all so much!"

J replied, "You've helped us out a lot. It's the least we can do."

Excited, Nika said, "Day one complete. How you feel Sasha?"

"I feel good, moderate pain, but I can handle it."

Walking to the door Nika said, "Okay great! Eat and get you some rest."

Sasha replied, "Will do. Thanks again Nika."

After Sasha showered and finished eating, she said to J, "Baby, let's get in these books before we go to bed.

Receptively, J said, "Okay baby."

The first book they read was on how to strengthen prayer life, so they went into the guest room closet. Sasha began to write her prayers down and tape them to the wall.

Her prayer said, "Come to me daily Lord. Whisper what you want and need me to do during this journey. I know that everyday isn't going to be a good one, so for those days Lord give me the extra wisdom to know what and how to handle it. When I feel I want to fall off Lord, pick me up and bring me back to where I need to be, for often times my flesh is weak. Help my mind to overpower it, amen."

J wrote on his card, "Lord… as a man, give me the strength to always be the man I need to be. When I'm weak, direct me to the right path to your strength. Give me the wisdom to know all the right words to say. In times that I'm speechless, direct my path in all the right directions and when hard times arrive, give me the strength to continue walking in your name, amen."

After almost forty-five minutes in their prayer

closet, they got up to go to bed. Sasha had fallen asleep in J's lap.

J said, "Baby! Baby! Wake up so we can go to bed."

Sasha replied "Okay baby."

Day Two

Knock. Knock.

Nika walked in and said, "Good Morning love. I know I'm early, but we have to get you back active soon."

Sasha responded, "Okay, where did J go?"

Nika answered, "He told me to tell you he'd be back soon."

Concerned Sasha asked, "You think we can get me dressed without him?"

Nika replied, "Yes love. He took out this dress for you."

"That's fine and it makes it easy on us."

Sasha said, "You want me to wheel you to the hall, or do you want to walk there again today?" Nika asked.

"I'll let you wheel me to the hall today." Sasha replied.

"First I'm going to pray for you before we get started."

Nika said, "Lord God… today we lift Sasha's

legs up to you once again. Lord… let today be the last day she has therapy. Strengthen not only her legs, but her faith in you Lord God. Help me to help her with the best of my abilities. Let my hands be like yours and touch and make the pain go away right now Lord. Show up in our lives right now Lord. We are seeking your glory."

She began to speak in tongues.

"Be **present** right now Lord. Send chills down our body and let her walk again today. *Whew* Lord God. I feel you moving. I feel your presence. Jesus, thank you for your glory. Thank you for grace, thank you for favor, thank you Father GOD! In your son's name I pray, amen."

"*Whew* Sasha. I don't know if you felt it, but I felt Him move in us a while ago." Sasha replied, "I did too Nika! He told me to get up and walk."

Excitedly, Nika said, "Well get up Sasha!"

Sasha stood a little wobbly at first, but she walked as God told her to and she immediately began to cry and speak in tongues.

"Lord I thank you!"

She cried.

"Thank you, thank you, thank you! Oh Lord, you're such and awesome God!"

As Sasha cried out, the Lord spoke to her, "Now spread my word and bring those you love to me."

"Yes Lord! Yes Lord!" Sasha said.

"I told you God could do the impossible, and I came here today knowing that today was going to be my last day here because I believed in the power of Prayer." Nika said.

"I thank you too Nika because from day one your prayers have gotten me to where I am now. I'm so grateful that God brought you into our lives." Sasha replied.

"I'm grateful that God moved through me to get you closer to Him. Everything I do, God tells or sends me to do. I always believe that's why the blessings just keep pouring out. Even when the devil tries to steal my joy and I think about giving up, God shows up and blessings pour out to me."

Nika said with tears in her eyes, "Lord that was so powerful! I'm going to call J to see where he is and I want you to put the wheelchair in the living room. When he comes in, I'm going to walk to him." Sasha said excited.

"He's going to be so surprised and happy." Nika said smiling.

"Right! Let me call him."

Siri spoke, *"How can I help you today."*

"Call J."

"Calling J."

Ring. Ring. Ring.

"What's up baby girl!?" J answered.

"Baby, where are you?" Sasha asked.

"Around the corner. You okay?" J replied.

"Yes! I just want you here right now." Sasha said.

"You not sounding right… I'm pulling in the yard. I'll be in shortly." J replied. "Okay baby." Sasha said as she hung up.

J walked in the door and yelled, "Baby!"

"I'm in the living room love." Sasha yelled back.

"Okay." J said as he walked in the living room to Sasha standing by herself.

"Stay there J."

"But—" J tried to say.

Sasha began to walk to J and he began to get teary eyed as she made it to him. He hugged her tightly and began to cry.

"That was nobody but God baby! He healed your legs and let you walk again." J said with tears falling.

"You're right." Sasha said hugging him tighter.

He continued to cry and thank God for all He had done.

"Y'all, I'm going to get out of here and go take care of the house. J… since it didn't take me long, I'll move back to my old apartment because I cannot afford that house." Nika said sadly.

"Nika that house is yours! All you have to pay is bills. Actually, both of these houses are paid in full. When I sold the lot of drugs I had left, it gave me enough to pay both houses off and still have enough to live off of for the next five years. Sign these papers and take them to get the home in your name." J said.

Nika dropped to the ground crying tears of joy.

She shouted, "Lord I thank you! You're so mighty and powerful! I'm forever grateful God. Oh God, thank you! If I had two thousand tongues, I couldn't thank you enough."

Sasha went and grabbed Nika, hugged her and whispered, "You deserve it all. Thank you for everything."

Still with tears flowing she hugged J and said, "Thank you so much! You don't know how good it is to finally be proud to have something to leave to my kids when I leave this earth. Thank you so much!"

"No Nika, thank you for your many prayers. God spoke to me to do that and I listened. You're family to us now." J said.

Sasha said, "J… I'm ready to go see Roxy."

Nika and J both stopped and looked.

J replied, "Well let's go then baby."

Sasha said walking out the door, "God is telling

me that I need to go show her I'm alright and to forgive her, so that's what I'm going to do."

J said softly, "Whatever you need to do, I'm behind you— no questions asked." Sasha said smiling, "Thank you baby."

Grabbing her hand, J said, "Welcome love."

As they got in the car, Sasha called Roxy.

Ring. Ring. Ring.

Roxy answered, "Hey Sasha baby! How you doing?"

Sasha replied, "Hey aunty. Are you at the club?"

"Yes I'm here. Why you ask?" Roxy asked.

"I'll be there in just a minute." Sasha replied.

"Wok... is everything okay?" Roxy asked.

"Yes, everything is fine. Why you ask that?"

"Just making sure baby." Roxy replied.

"Alright, see you in a few." Sasha said.

"Alright, see you." Roxy replied as they hung up.

Sasha told J, "I think that she thinks that I'm after her."

"Why you think that?" J asked.

"She kept asking me 'was everything okay' like she was paranoid." Sasha said. "She'll see that you're not when we get there." J replied.

Pulling into the parking lot, Sasha asked, "Do you want to go in with me?"

J replied. "If you want me to I will."

"Please." Sasha said.

"Alright love. I'm behind you." J said opening the door.

Knock. Knock. Knock.

"Who is it?" Roxy yelled.

"It's Wok, aunty." Sasha replied.

"Come on in baby." Roxy said.

Sasha walked in and said, "Hey. Before I start, I'm not here in any way to get back at you for what happened."

Shocked, Roxy started crying.

She said, "Wok you're walking again! God really healed you didn't He?"

In reply Sasha said, "As a matter of fact, He did. If you let me help you, He can do the same for you."

Roxy said, "I'm sorry, but I think it's a little too late for me. I've did too many bad things for Him to help me."

Sasha replied, "It's not. God is a forgiving God. All you have to do is repent your sins and ask for forgiveness. Show God that you're trying to get it right with Him." With her head down Roxy said, "I don't even know how to start Wok."

Sasha said softly, "I'll help you get down on

your knees and say these things." Roxy got on her knees and repeated Sasha, "Lord, today I come to you a lost soul going in all the wrong directions. I need your guidance Lord. Show me how to be a better person. I repent all my sins to you. Please forgive me for my past and help me to achieve a better future. Oh God I apologize for all the times I failed you. In Jesus' name I pray, amen."

Sasha then said, "Come here J. Let's pray over Roxy."

J came and they began to pray.

Sasha spoke in tongues and J said, "Lord touch right now. Show your presence to a lost soul. Speak to her right now. Shower down your love on her right now Lord. As we touch and agree, let your power flow through us. Help us to get Roxy delivered from all the evil stored in her. Any malicious energy in her, release it right now! Make her whole again. In your name we pray, amen."

Crying Roxy said, "Amen, amen, amen! Thank you, Lord!"

She began to speak in tongues.

"Lord I thank you for showing me that you are indeed real!"

Sasha grabbed Roxy and said, "Aunty, let me help you get closer to God."

Roxy replied, "I am and I will baby. I promise."

Sasha said smiling, "I love you aunty. We gonna get out of here. You should come over tomorrow or something."

With tears in her eyes Roxy said, "I love you too Wok and I'll call you tomorrow." Sasha replied, "Okay, see you later."

As J and Sasha walked out, J said, "I really surprised myself in there. God is really working with me because that prayer came directly from Him and I felt some things come from Roxy in that room."

Sasha replied, "She had a spiritual baptism. God cleansed both yours and Roxy's soul. From here you have to continue to strengthen your faith baby." J replied.

"I plan to baby and I want to take it to the streets. I want to save souls on these street corners for dudes that I used to be."

Sasha said smiling, "Baby whatever you do, I'm there. I got your back through any fight. Let's help some people change their lives around."

About the Author

SHATERRA J. GENTRY was born and raised in a small country town called McNab, AR. She is a single mother of a beautiful four-year-old daughter who is the reason for all of her accomplishments. She is a graduate from Saratoga High School. She accomplished two years of college in General Studies. Shaterra enjoys making others smile and encouraging others. Above all, she keeps God first in all things that she does! Shaterra lives by Jeremiah 29:11.

Also Available from
J. Kenkade Publishing

A best-seller. A Powerful, life-changing truth of the spiritual and emotional struggles of women and girls. With the guidance of the Holy Spirit, DIVAS Unchained exposes Satan's lies and strongholds that our women and girls have been enchained to, reveals what's been holding them back, and provides them with the tools to pull down every stronghold.

Also Available from
J. Kenkade Publishing

ISBN: 978-1-944486-13-6
Purchase at www.jkenkade.com

Captivating. Step into the life story of a young girl tormented by an abusive family. Young Cindy rewrites her experiences with a mother introduced to drugs, sexual abuse from her father, and death. Cindy reveals how strong God can make anyone in the midst of Satan's schemes. Experience her journey in "Revealing the Secrets of My Hurt."

Also Available from
J. Kenkade Publishing